PUFFIN BOOKS

Last Bus

Robert Swindells left school at the age of fifteen and joined the Royal Air Force at $17^1/_2$. After his discharge, he worked at a variety of jobs, before training and working as a teacher. He is now a full-time writer and lives with his wife Brenda on the Yorkshire moors. Robert Swindells has written many books for young people, and in 1984 was the winner of the Children's Book Award and the Other Award for his novel *Brother in the Land*. He won the Children's Book Award for a second time in 1990 with *Room 13*, and in 1994 *Stone Cold* won the Carnegie Medal and the Sheffield Children's Book Award.

SURFERS

LAST BUS

Robert Swindells

Illustrated by

Mark Edwards

PUFFIN BOOKS

PUFFIN BOOKS

Published by the Penguin Group
Penguin Books Ltd, 27 Wrights Lane, London W8 5TZ, England
Penguin Putnam Inc., 375 Hudson Street, New York, New York 10014, USA
Penguin Books Australia Ltd, Ringwood, Victoria, Australia
Penguin Books Canada Ltd, 10 Alcorn Avenue, Toronto, Ontario, Canada M4V 3B2
Penguin Books (NZ) Ltd, 182–190 Wairau Road, Auckland 10, New Zealand

Penguin Books Ltd, Registered Offices: Harmondsworth, Middlesex, England

First published by Hamish Hamilton Ltd, 1996
Published in Puffin Books 1997
7

Text copyright © Robert Swindells, 1996
Illustrations copyright © Mark Edwards, 1996
All rights reserved

The moral right of the authors and illustrator has been asserted

Filmset in Bembo

Made and printed in England by Clays Ltd, St Ives plc

British Library Cataloguing in Publication Data
A CIP catalogue record for this book is available from the British Library

ISBN 0–140–37971–1

Contents

1	The Snag	1
2	Anywhere	7
3	Ducks	12
4	Walk, Don't Run	17
5	My Cow	25
6	White-Knuckle Ride	32
7	Tarantula	40
8	My Young Day	46
9	Yarbles!	52
10	Old Myself Someday	59
11	Intergalactic	65
12	No Can Do	70
13	Another Comedian	77
14	Someone Else's Dream	84

Chapter One
The Snag

"SATURDAY TOMORROW," SAID Andy.

Chris nodded. "Yeah."

"What you doing, then?"

"What — tomorrow?"

"No, next Pancake Tuesday, you dip-stick. Of *course* tomorrow."

"Oh, I dunno. Mum and Dad'll be off to the garden centre, I expect. I might go with them."

Andy shot his companion a sideways glance. "*Garden* centre – how d'you stand the excitement?"

Chris shrugged. "I know, but . . . well, what *else* is there to do if you don't want to gawp at the telly all day?"

"Millions of things. We could go down Fagley Woods, look for conkers."

"I'm not allowed."

"Not *allowed*?"

"In the woods, no. Dad says it's dangerous. Funny people about. You know?"

"Well yeah, but you're *eleven* for pete's sake, not six. What does he think's going to happen to you?"

"Don't ask me. You know what dads are like."

They walked on for a while without speaking, their school bags bouncing on their shoulders. They were classmates, just starting to be friends. After a while Andy said, "Do you ever ride the buses, Chris?"

"Buses?" Chris shook his head. "We go everywhere in the car."

Andy chuckled. "So do we, but there's a snag, isn't there?"

"What snag?"

"Well, think about it."

"I don't know what you're on about, Andy."

Andy grinned. "Can you go in the car by yourself?"

"'Course not, and neither can you."

"Well then, that's the snag. Go by car,

3

you've got the wrinklies on your back. Lot of stuff you can't *do*, know what I mean?"

Chris looked at him. "What sort of stuff?"

"Oh, all sorts. Shopping, for instance."

"*Shopping*? I shop with my folks all the time."

Andy laughed. "Not like I mean. You shop with your folks, you *pay*, right?"

"Well yeah . . ." Chris stared. "D'you mean . . . ?"

Andy nodded. "'Course. It's easy, Chris. Dead easy. I do it all the time."

"Yeah, but like – if you get caught . . ."

"You don't *get* caught, you turkey, that's the whole point. There's cameras and security guys and you beat the lot of 'em. It's something to *do*, you know?

Something exciting."

Chris shook his head. "Not for me. I'd rather be bored."

Andy shrugged. "You will be, then."

There was another silence. They were coming to Aspen Way, where Andy lived. Chris's place, Oak Crescent, was further on. At the corner Chris said, "What did you mean about the buses? Riding the buses?"

Andy looked at him. "D'you know what a Day Rover is?"

"No."

"It's a ticket. Costs two-fifty and lasts one day, but you can take as many bus rides as you want that day. I've been all over. Miles out of town in every direction. It's great."

"Well . . ." Chris pulled a face. "Can't

5

we do that tomorrow without – you know – without *shopping*?"

Andy grinned. "Sure, if you like. Do you have two-fifty?"

"I can get it."

"OK. I'll see you here at nine in the morning, then."

"Do I need to bring anything – a sandwich, drink?"

Andy shook his head. "Naw. We'll manage." He smiled. "See you later."

Chris nodded. "Nine on the dot."

Chapter Two
Anywhere

"So." CHRIS'S MOTHER smiled brightly across the breakfast table. "Any plans, love? For the day I mean?"

Chris nodded. "I'm meeting Andy, Mum. Nine o'clock, to ride the buses."

"What d'you mean, ride the buses?"

"We're getting Day Rovers and riding around. You know – anywhere."

His mother pulled a face. "Funny idea. And who's Andy?"

"Andy Bulmer. Guy in my class. Lives on Aspen Way."

She frowned. "Wasn't he in trouble a while back truanting or something? The name's familiar."

"Well yes, but he's OK now, Mum, honestly. Hasn't bunked off for yonks."

"Hmmm, well. Your dad and I don't want you getting in with the wrong crowd, Chris, that's all. You can go, but don't let this boy lead you astray, will you? I mean, don't go doing bad things or silly things just because Andy suggests them."

"'Course not, Mum." The word 'shopping' came into his head and he felt himself blushing. "I told you – we'll just be riding buses. Can't go far wrong there, can we?"

"I certainly hope not, dear. Do you expect to be home for lunch?"

"No. Andy said all day, I think."

"Ah, well – you're to be back by six at the latest, Chris." She gazed at him. "At the *latest*, d'you hear?"

"Yes, Mum."

It was two minutes to nine when he reached the end of Aspen Way. Andy was there in his jacket, jeans and trainers. His bag was on his back. Chris looked at it. "You said not to bring anything."

Andy grinned. "Relax, kid, it's empty."

"So why . . . ?"

"Might come in handy, that's all. Got the fare?"

"Sure."

"Let's go then."

They walked the half mile to the bus station, bought tickets and looked around. There were plenty of buses to choose from.

"That's a good one," said Andy. "662. Goes out Cramlington way. You been there?"

"Through it," said Chris, "in the car."

Andy nodded. "This'll do for starters, then. Come on." They boarded the double decker, flashed their Rovers and went upstairs. There were a few passengers but the front seats were empty. The two boys grabbed them and gazed down on the morning bustle till the driver started his engine and released the brake. The bus growled forward, shuddering. Andy grinned and whispered:

"Got my ticket
Paid my fare
Where it takes me
I don't care."

Chris glanced sideways at his friend and could tell by the look on his face that he really didn't.

Chapter Three
Ducks

CRAMLINGTON. THE BUS swung into its turning circle and stopped under some sycamores. It was twenty past ten. "This is it," said Andy. "Terminus. Come on."

They were the only passengers left on the top deck. They clattered down the stairs. An old woman was getting off. She was the last. The driver sat back, lighting a cigarette. Andy looked at him. "What time d'you go back?"

"Half past."

"What about the one after that?"

"Leaves here at ten to eleven."

"Thanks."

It was a cool morning, but bright. The two boys sauntered through the village. There was a bench by a pond. They sat down. Some ducks left the water and waddled up to them. "They're hungry," said Chris. "Wish I'd brought a sandwich now."

Andy stood up. "Wait here. I won't be a minute."

Across the pond was a willow tree. Its slim leaves were turning yellow. Each time the breeze stirred the branches a shower of leaves fell fluttering on to the water. Winter soon, thought Chris. Wonder what the ducks do when the pond freezes over. The birds, disappointed at receiving no food, were moving away.

"Here y'are." Andy plumped down beside him. "Sticky buns." There were two, wrapped in tissue paper. He handed one to Chris.

"Where'd you get 'em?"

"Hairdresser's," said Andy. "Where d'you think?"

"Bread shop?"

"Right." He tore lumps off his bun and lobbed them towards the ducks. Chris did the same. The ducks squabbled. More appeared from under the willow, paddling frantically towards the feast. Chris chucked a fistful of crumbs in the pond. The flotilla converged like piranhas on a bleeding swimmer. In half a minute all the bread had gone.

Andy balled up the tissue, wiped his fingers with it and dropped it in a wire basket beside the bench. A duck bustled up and pecked the mesh. Andy laughed. "It's paper, greedy-guts."

"The buns didn't last long," said Chris. "How much were they?"

"Not a lot. Come on."

They mooched about Cramlington till they saw the bus come through, then walked up to the terminus and caught it. Front seats again, upstairs. When they were settled, Chris looked at Andy. "Those buns," he said. "Did you . . . ?"

"Look, don't *worry*, OK? Just relax, enjoy the ride." Andy sat back smiling. "We'll try the 664 next I think. Troydale. Good place to get lunch."

Chapter Four
Walk, Don't Run

THE 664 WAS ready to go when they got back to the bus station. "Our lucky day," grinned Andy, but the bus was nearly full. They got the last two seats downstairs, which weren't together.

At the first stop two women got on

17

with shopping bags. Chris gave up his seat. Andy closed his eyes and pretended he hadn't seen the women so one of them had to stand. Her friend put both sets of bags on the floor between her feet, and they swapped places after three or four stops.

Nearing Troydale the bus half emptied and there was no problem. Chris slipped into a vacant double and Andy joined him.

"You're barmy," he smiled.

"How d'you mean?"

"Giving up your seat. You've paid, same as everybody else. You're entitled to sit."

"Well, I know, but they had shopping. Heavy bags."

"So what? They could see the bus was full before they got on. They should've waited for the next if they didn't want to stand."

"But what if the *next* was full as well?"

Andy shrugged. "Not your problem, mate."

"Well, I was being polite, that's all."

"You were being a div."

Troydale was bigger than Cramlington. A town rather than a village. There was no pond but there was a square with seats round a war memorial and scavenging pigeons. They sat down. Andy nodded towards the pigeons. "Fancy feeding 'em, do you?"

"N – no!" Not with stolen buns, Chris thought but didn't say. Andy shrugged. "Suit yourself."

They had an hour before catching the

bus back. They watched people and pigeons till a church clock somewhere chimed. Andy looked at his watch and stood up. "Come on, Chris. Quarter past twelve. Time for a spot of lunch."

They walked along the high street till they came to a bread shop with a cafe. *Lite-bite*, said the sign. "This'll do nicely," said Andy.

"I . . . I haven't much dosh," stammered Chris.

"Don't worry."

They went through the shop to the cafe area. Chris headed for the first table but Andy grabbed his shoulder. "Not there, you spasmo. Over here." They sat down. Chris looked at his friend. "What was wrong with . . . ?"

"It was for two."

"But we *are* two, Andy."

"Yeah, I *know*, but . . . oh, never mind. You'll see."

A waitress came. "Sausage, egg and chips," said Andy. "Oh – and a Coke. And the same for my mum please, except she'll have tea instead of the Coke." He smiled. "She'll be along in a minute – she's at the hairdresser's."

The girl looked at Chris. He scanned the menu, his mind racing. What was Andy *up* to? *Was* his mum here in Troydale? He hadn't mentioned it. Perhaps she'd arranged to meet her son for lunch?

"I – I'll just have . . ."

Andy chuckled. "He'll have the same as me, love."

"*Andy* . . . ?"

"Look – relax, OK? *Mummy's* paying."

"Mummy?" Chris stared at his companion as the girl moved away. "Whose mummy are you on about, Andy?"

"Ah, well." Andy grinned at the table-top. "That's the sixty-four thousand dollar question, isn't it?"

The food came. They ate and drank. Andy polished off most of his own lunch, then started on his mother's. He was obviously enjoying the food, but Chris wasn't. He couldn't, for wondering what his companion was playing at. I bet he intends doing a runner, he thought. Dashing out without paying. I'll *die* if he does. *And* I'll get caught. He groaned, imagining his parents collecting him from the police station.

Andy glanced up.

"What's up *now*?"

"This." Chris indicated his plate. "Have you got the dosh to pay for this lot, 'cause *I* haven't."

"Oh, for pete's sake stop fretting and get stuck in. I *told* you – Mummy'll see to it."

When they'd finished, Andy murmured, "Get up and walk out. Take your time. Wait outside."

"But . . . ?"

"Just *do* it."

To his surprise, nobody challenged him. No mother had turned up so he assumed Andy meant to make a dash for it. He loitered on the pavement ready to run, wishing he'd gone to the garden centre. Through the plate glass window he saw Andy shove his chair back and stand up. This is it, he told himself, but before Andy could make his move the waitress was beside him. Chris gaped. "Oh God," he whispered, "they've got him. We've had it."

Andy didn't look worried. He was talking to the girl, smiling, nodding towards a woman buying bread at the counter. The waitress glanced at the woman and nodded. Andy smiled and walked towards the exit. Passing the counter he spoke to the woman, who glanced towards the approaching waitress. The two converged as Andy left the shop. "Come on," he hissed. "Into the crowd, but *walk*, don't run."

Chapter Five
My Cow

"THAT WOMAN," SAID Chris, as the two boys emerged from an alley and turned right into a stream of shoppers. "She wasn't your . . ."

"'*Course* not, you airhead. She was about the right age though, and the waitress didn't see her come in." Andy winked. "You've got to *think* of these things, see, or it doesn't work."

"We left her to pay for three meals, Andy – a complete stranger!"

"Naw!" Andy shook his head. "She won't pay, Chris. She'll say she's not our mother, that's all. There's nothing they can do."

"The waitress, then – what if *she* has to pay? What if they stop it out of her wages?"

Andy grinned. "She doesn't *need* wages, does she, now that she knows how to eat for free."

Chris didn't reply. He was going off Andy. If he'd had any dosh he'd have gone back to the cafe, owned up and paid. He couldn't do that, but he could split up with Andy as soon as they were back in town.

The bus was seven minutes late and when it came it was a single decker. They sat on the long seat at the back. Andy knew something was wrong. He kept trying to start conversations but Chris only grunted, staring out of the window.

In the bus station Chris said, "I''d better go. Mum'll be –"

"Look – there's a 660 in," Andy interrupted.

Chris looked. "Applebeck. How far's that?"

"Oh – five, six miles. Say half an hour."

"What's there?"

Andy shrugged. "Shops. Houses. All the usual stuff. It's a nice run though – country lanes."

"And we won't — you know — cheat anybody or anything like that?"

Andy laughed. "You're a boyscout, Chris, d'you know that? A real boy-scout." He shook his head. "No, we won't cheat anybody if you'd rather not. Come on."

Front seats again, upstairs. It *was* a nice run. Pretty scenery, not many stops. They were in Applebeck by five past two. It was sunny but clouds were rolling in from the west. The main street was lined with stalls, selling just about everything you could think of. "Market day. My favourite," said Andy.

Chris shot him a look. "You're not going to . . . ?"

"No — I *promised*, didn't I?" He smiled. "Ever seen 'em selling cows and stuff?"

Chris looked blank. "What — on stalls?"

"No, you plonker. At auction."

"No."

"Well, you're about to." He led the way towards a long brick building on the edge of town. In front of the building were some pens made of tubular metal. Sheep and cows stood in some of them. Men with sticks leaned on the pens, ignoring the drizzle, talking. Andy headed for a doorway with a sign over it.

APPLEBECK AUCTION MART

Chris trotted after him. "Are we allowed in here, Andy?"

"'Course. Loads of people come in just to get out of the rain."

Inside, tiers of rough benches were ranged round a railed square with a cement floor. The two boys sat down on one of the benches. A man was walking a black and white cow round and round the square while another man talked about it. A few farmers leaned on the rail, watching the cow. After a minute the bidding began.

Chris couldn't make out what was happening. Andy raised a finger and nodded. The auctioneer paused momentarily in his patter, then continued. Andy chuckled. "See that? That was my cow for a second or two."

Chris looked at him. "You – *bought* it?"

"*Bid* for it, yeah. Forty quid, I think."

"But – have you *got* forty pounds?"

"Have I thump!"

"So what if – you know – nobody topped your bid?"

"What – forty quid? No chance." He grinned. "If it *did* happen I'd have to leg it. Can't see my dad letting me keep a flipping *cow* in my room."

Chris shook his head. "You've done it before, haven't you?"

Andy nodded. "Loads of times. Sheep, pigs, cows. I owned this whacking great bull for a second once – a Charolais. You should've seen it."

Chris shook his head again. "You're nuts, Andy. Out of your tree. I mean it."

They stayed twenty minutes or so, then Andy stood up. "Seen one cow, you seen 'em all," he said. "Let's go."

Chapter Six
White-Knuckle Ride

"OH, CRIKEY!" CHRIS turned away from the timetable bolted to the bus-stop. "We've just missed one. There isn't another for fifty-five minutes."

Andy shook his head. "No good. We won't fit another ride in if we wait for that. We'll have to twoc."

"Twoc – what's that?"

"Oh, it's . . . hitching a ride, sort of. Yeah. That's what it is. Follow your Uncle Andy."

They walked back the way they'd come. It had stopped raining. Across the road from the auction mart was a pub called The Drovers. Andy crossed with Chris on his heels. Most of the vehicles in the car park were four-wheel drive jobs, spattered with mud. Some were hitched to trailers.

Andy looked at Chris. "All these belong to farmers, right?" He nodded towards the pub. "They're in there, swilling and stuffing. All *you*'ve got to do is watch that door and give me a yell if anybody comes out." He fished in his bag and produced a strip of parcel strapping and a length of wire.

"Wh . . . what are *you* going to do, Andy?"

"Borrow one of these."

"You mean nick one, don't you?"

"Naw. I said borrow and I mean borrow. We're not going to sell the thing or wreck it. They'll find it in Cranley without a scratch on it. How can that be stealing?"

Chris shook his head. "Count me out, Andy. I won't watch the door for you, and I won't ride in a stolen car. You're under-age anyway! I'm off."

Andy shrugged. "Suit yourself. Walk home for all I care, but it's going to rain again any minute." He turned, passing from sight between two vehicles.

Chris hurried out of the car park and started walking. He didn't fancy trekking five miles, but he daren't hang about in Applebeck. Andy was sure to be caught, and somebody might remember seeing them together.

Andy was right about the rain though. It started before Chris had gone a hundred metres. He put his collar up and his head down and trudged on, hands in pockets.

He'd been walking about ten minutes when he heard a motor behind. There was no pavement, so he stepped on to the verge and looked back. It was a four by four towing a trailer. As it drew near the driver flashed his lights and slowed, then leaned across and stuck his head out. It was Andy, grinning. "Can I drop you somewhere?"

Chris shook his head and walked on. The vehicle crawled past him and stopped. He looked up. A cow gazed at him from the trailer. He lowered his head and put on a spurt to pass the vehicle.

"Hey, boy scout." Chris glanced sideways into Andy's mocking face. "Nobody's chasing me. No hassle. I'll be in Cranley in five minutes, nice and dry. You'll have four miles to walk and be soaking wet. Come on – hop in."

Well, why the heck not? Chris asked himself. As Andy says, no one's chasing and I'm getting drowned. He nodded.

Andy's grin broadened. He let his friend slide in, then shot away before he had time to close the door. Tarmac, verge and hedge blurred by. With a yelp of alarm, Chris slammed the door and clung to the edges of his seat as they careered along the lane, swinging and bouncing. "Hey, steady on!" he gasped. "You'll lose the flipping trailer at this rate."

"Well," drawled Andy, hunched over the wheel. "Cow can probably use a bit of excitement." He smiled. "It's a boring old life you know, being a cow."

They weren't in Cranley in five minutes. It took seven, and they didn't go right in. Andy steered the vehicle into a cul-de-sac on the new trading estate, and they got out. Chris was anxious to leave the scene, but Andy was in no hurry. "Only draw attention to yourself, rushing," he said. He strolled back to the horse box and peered in. "Enjoy that, did you, cow? It's what's known as a white-knuckle ride." He chuckled. "Life on the farm's never going to be the same for you, is it?"

They walked away. The trading estate was deserted at weekends.

"What about the cow?" asked Chris. "It could starve to death before anybody finds it."

Andy shrugged. "Phone sombody if you're bothered. The R.S.P.C.A. or something." He grinnned wickedly. "Anyone but the police."

They strolled into town. Chris found a phone box. The R.S.P.C.A. didn't answer so he called the local newspaper and told them where the cow was. The woman asked his name. Bart Simpson, he said, and hung up. He'd intended splitting up with Andy, going home early, but he was enjoying himself in a funny way. It had been scary but it had been fun too. So. One more ride, eh? They headed for the bus station.

Chapter Seven
Tarantula

"So where now?" asked Chris.

"We'll catch the 661, get off in Barmston. There's a terrific pet shop there — snakes, terrapins, piranhas — you name it. Last time they had a tarantula."

"A *tarantula*?"

"Yeah, in a tank. You should've seen it, Chris — it was this big."

"When was this?" Chris had never seen a tarantula.

"Oh — two, three weeks back," said Andy.

Chris shook his head. "It'll have gone by now."

Andy chuckled. "I doubt it. They were asking three hundred quid for it."

"Three hundred pounds for a *spider*?"

"Ah, but *what* a spider, Chris. It was like a boxing glove with legs."

Chris looked at him. "Say you won't nick it, Andy. Say you won't nick *anything*. It *really* screws me up, your thieving."

"You have my word, OK?" said Andy with an innocent look.

★

They got the 661. It was another single decker, and it was packed when they reached Barmston, which wasn't the terminus. A few passengers got off with them, but there were just as many getting on.

"Phew!" Andy fanned himself as they stepped down. "What a crush, eh? Nice to be out of it."

"We'd better give ourselves plenty of time when we're leaving," said Chris, "if that's how full they get."

"Don't worry," nodded Andy, "we will."

There was no tarantula. Chris suspected there never had been, but it *was* a terrific pet shop. It was huge – more like a supermarket, though not as brightly lit. They sauntered up and down the aisles. Some were lined with bubbling tanks in which fish darted like sprays of multi-coloured gems. Others led between stacks of small cages with chipmunks, rats and hamsters. Larger cages held guinea pigs, chinchillas and rabbits. There was a reptile section where grass snakes, mambas, geckos and boa-constrictors lay basking in the heat from powerful lamps. They saw locusts, silkworms and stick-insects. There was even a tank of scorpions, but the most popular aisles – the aisles where you had to push and shove to get by – were those where pups and kittens were displayed.

The pair had negotiated these and were browsing among the birds when the public address system crackled and a voice said, "Ladies and gentlemen, this store will close in fifteen minutes. Fifteen minutes. Thank you."

Chris looked at his watch. It was a quarter to five. "Come on," he said, "I'm supposed to be home by six."

Andy nodded. "No prob. It's this way."

He led Chris out to the street. It was drizzling. Andy glanced at Chris.

"Some place, huh?"

"Yes." Chris strode out, anxious to be at the bus stop.

Andy lagged half a pace behind, trotting to keep up. "Slow down, can't you?" he grumbled. "It's not the flipping marathon."

They hurried along the wet street, hands in pockets, shoulders hunched. Coming in sight of the bus stop, Chris gasped in dismay. There was a queue of at least twenty people. The boys tagged on the end. Chris sighed. "I just hope it's not already packed when it gets here."

Andy nodded. "Me too. Don't want this little fella squashed, do we?"

"Huh?" Chris peered at his companion through rain-beaded lashes and saw a small lump in Andy's leather jacket. As Chris stared, a tiny head appeared in the vee above the zipper. Wide blue eyes gazed out. The kitten mewed weakly as a raindrop hit its nose.

Chapter Eight
My Young Day

"YOU SAID YOU wouldn't nick anything,"
cried Chris. "You *promised*."

"I didn't *mean* to nick it, Chris, but it
looked at me — you know, like it was saying *get me out of here*, and I . . . well, it felt
more like rescuing than stealing."

"But what if . . . I mean, won't your parents wonder where you got it?"

"I'll say I found it in an alleyway, wet and starving." He winked. "They'll have to let me keep it then."

Chris sighed. "Do you lie to your folks a lot, Andy?"

"Oh, yeah. You have to, don't you? No peace otherwise."

"*I* don't. I'm no good at it. They'd know." He looked at his watch. "Bus is late. No chance of being home for six now."

Andy shrugged. "Not your fault if the bus runs late, is it?"

Chris pulled a face. "My folks won't see it like that, Andy. They'll say I should've got an earlier one."

It was raining harder. Andy shoved the

kitten's head inside his jacket and zipped it up. Street lights were coming on. Traffic swished by and sprayed the queue, which was longer now. Chris's hair was plastered to his skull. Water was streaming down his neck. He pulled out his handkerchief and mopped his head. He was about to ask Andy how much it would cost to get a taxi when a man in front of them grunted, "Here it comes — better late than never," and an old double decker came growling up.

The queue shuffled forward. Umbrellas were furled and shaken. People groped in soggy pockets for change. The man in front of Chris and Andy reached the front and stepped up, out of the rain. The driver was taking money, issuing tickets. It was a slow process.

The boys stood at the kerb, poised to board. Presently the man ahead of them took a pace forward and the pair found a precarious foothold on the step. The driver issued one more ticket, then leaned across and thrust his arm between them and the man in front. "Full up," he grunted. "There's another one behind." Clucks and groans rose from those still queueing.

"How far behind?" demanded Andy.

The driver glared. "Twenty minutes. Come on now – off my bus – I'm running late as it is."

"We'd noticed," shouted someone in the queue. The two boys stepped back off the platform, over the swirling gutter and on to the kerb. The laden bus lurched away with a crash of gears in a gout of blue pollution.

Chris groaned. "Twenty minutes." He looked at Andy. "I'd better call home. Will you save my place while I go and find a phone?"

Andy nodded. "Sure. Why don't you have 'em drive out and pick us up?"

"Phoooh!" Chris shook his head. "You don't know my dad. I can just imagine what he'd say. *You got yourself out there – it's up to you to get yourself back.* He's a prince among men, my dad."

"It's 'cause you don't *lie* to him enough," growled Andy.

Chris couldn't find a phone that worked. He tried four and they were all vandalized. Afraid he'd miss the bus, he returned to the queue and reported his failure. Andy shook his head. "I don't know what the world's coming to," he

said in an old man voice. "All this dis-
honesty. Not like when I was a boy." He
grabbed hold of Chris's sleeve and gazed
into his eyes. "D'you know, lad, in my
young day you could leave a wallet full of
fivers on a wall and it'd still be there
when you came back for it ten hours
later." He laughed. "Yep — folks were *seriously* thick in the good old days."

Chris smiled faintly. In happier cir-
cumstances he'd have laughed out loud,
but he wasn't in the mood. It was twenty
to six. He was cold, wet and hungry. He
wished the bus would hurry up and
come. At least they were first in the
queue, so they'd get on all right. Unless it
drove past full, of course.

Chapter Nine
Yarbles!

THE BUS DROVE past flashing its lights – a sort of apology. You could see it was packed but the dripping queue glared after its tail lights, muttering. "That's it," said Chris, turning from the kerb. "I'm off to find a taxi."

Andy shook his head. "Taxi from here'll cost a fortune and you've got no dosh."

"No, but *you* have, and I've got a bit. We could put it together and I'll pay you back on Monday."

"No way. Taxis rob you. They're all crooks."

"Look who's talking!" blurted Chris, before he could stop himself. "You've nicked two sticky buns, three dinners, a cow and a kitten, and that's just *today*. God knows what your score is for the year."

"God knows, does He?" grinned Andy, unfazed. "Why hasn't He struck me dead then, kiddo?"

Chris looked at him. "Just because He hasn't yet doesn't mean He won't. I hope

I'm not standing next to you when it happens, that's all."

"Yarbles!"

Stuck without his companion's money, Chris subsided and stood gazing down the road. He'd resigned himself to another twenty minutes, but in fact a bus appeared in less than five. "Hey, amazing," he said, but as it drew near he saw that it wasn't a 661. He squinted at Andy through his sodden fringe. "Where's the 666 go?"

Andy shrugged. "Search me. Doesn't matter – it's pointing in the right direction and we'll be dry and warm."

"Yeah, but . . ."

"Don't worry – I'll ask."

The vehicle shuddered to a halt. Its door hissed open. "Room for two standing," barked the driver. "Two only."

Cries of anger and dismay rose from the queue as the boys boarded. "Going to Cranley, are you?" asked Andy, flashing his ticket.

The driver nodded. "This'll take you where you're bound, lad." He glanced in his mirror. "Move right down the car, please. Hold tight."

There was a rail to hold on to. Puddles formed round their feet as the bus jerked and shuddered its way out of Barmston on to a narrow, unlit road. With his free hand Chris fished out the sodden hanky and wiped his head, face and neck. It felt good not being rained on. Andy's hand cradled the kitten, which was mewing weakly inside his jacket.

A seated woman looked up. A large

handbag rested in her lap. "What you got in there, son?"

"Kitten," said Andy.

"Oh – poor little thing. Yours, is it?"

"No, it belongs to the Prime flippin' Minister." He glared at the woman. "'*Course* it's mine, you daft cow."

"No need to talk like *that*," spluttered the woman. "I only asked." Andy didn't reply but looked past the woman's head, out of the window.

A man standing next to him was giggling. "Daft cow," he tittered. "Nice one, that."

Andy glared at him. The guy had a green badge on his lapel with the word ESCORT on it. Andy frowned. Escort . . . ?

Chris was mortified by his companion's

rudeness. He felt like apologizing for Andy, but that might start him off again. He'd have liked to pretend they weren't together, but everybody had seen them get on. He ignored Andy, avoiding his eyes by studying the passengers he could see.

They were steaming. They'd all been rained on, it was warm in the bus and steam was rising from their clothes. They were a mixed bunch — businessmen, housewives, workers, down and outs. There were no kids apart from themselves, and there wasn't much chat. A sign said NO SMOKING, but a man leaned forward and called to the driver, "All right if I smoke, squire?"

The driver eyeballed him in the mirror. "Plenty of time to smoke when you get off." He smiled as though at some private joke. "Squire."

The man muttered something and sat back, fiddling with his Marlboro pack.

The giggler was at it again. "When you get off," he chuckled. "Smoke when you get off. It's the way they tell 'em that gets me."

Chapter Ten
Old Myself Someday

CHRIS WATCHED THE giggler through the corner of his eye. What had the driver said that was funny, for crying out loud? *Plenty of time to smoke when you get off.* Yet he'd smiled saying it, and this dork was practically killing himself. Chris didn't particularly want to speak to the guy, but curiosity got the better of him and he said, "I don't get it."

The man looked at him. "Wh–what don't you get, kiddo?"

"What the driver said. I don't see anything funny in it."

"Oh well, no, you won't." The guy wiped his eyes with the knuckles of his free hand. "You won't, because you haven't travelled on this bus before."

"How do you know? And what's that got to do with it anyway?"

The man chuckled. "It's got *everything* to do with it, believe me. And as to how I know . . . look." He pulled out the lapel with the badge. "I'm the escort."

"What's *that* mean?"

The man shrugged. "I escort folks to

their destination. It's my job."

"Do you . . . live in Cranley, then?"

"Huh? Oh no. No. Used to, not any more."

"Ah." Chris smiled. "You've moved away, eh? Somewhere a bit warmer, maybe."

"Somewhere a bit . . ." A whoop began. The guy slapped a hand over his mouth and dissolved into fits of laughter, shaking as the tears streamed down his cheeks. "Somewhere . . . a bit . . . somewhere a bit warmer," he choked. "Ooooh, you're a pair, you and that driver. You want to get together, form a double act." He hung shaking from the rail, helpless with mirth.

Chris felt himself blush. Everybody was staring. Twisting round in their seats, looking for the joke. Andy growled, "What's up with *him*?"

Chris shrugged. "Dunno. Nutcase, I guess. Laughs at nowt."

He bent forward to peer through the window, seeing mostly reflections. "Any idea where we are?"

Andy looked out. "Not exactly. Bit to go yet, I think."

"Yeah."

They seemed to be on a long, shallow downslope. Chris frowned, trying to remember the 661 climbing a hill like this. He'd feel happier if he could, but he couldn't. He pulled a face. Wish we'd come to some lights so I can see out, he thought, and when's somebody going to get off so we can at least sit down?

Nobody was showing any sign of

getting off. Once the giggler went quiet everybody looked straight in front, seemingly absorbed with their thoughts. Maybe there are very few houses between Barmston and Cranley, he mused. He wished he'd taken more notice on the outward journey.

"Hey, son." Chris felt a tug on the back of his jacket and turned.

A wrinkled old man was looking up at him through red-rimmed, watery eyes.

"What?"

"Ask the driver for another chance."

"What?"

"Another chance. You never know."

"Oh, right." He smiled, nodded and turned away. Another flipping nutcase. Why do I attract 'em?

He hoped the old crackpot wouldn't

persist, but no such luck. Tug. "Son?" Pause. Tug. "Sonny?" Louder.

Chris spun round, irritation smothering compassion. "Leave me alone," he snapped. "Keep your hands to yourself and mind your own business."

The old man gazed up, hurt in his eyes. "I was . . . I'm trying to . . ." He shook his head. "Never mind, it doesn't matter."

Chris turned his back, thinking: he's harmless, poor old guy. I should've humoured him instead of biting his head off. I'll be old myself someday. Impulsively he turned, squeezed the old man's shoulder and said, "I'm sorry. I shouldn't have yelled. I'll be old myself someday."

The man glanced up. "Oh *will* you, son?" he croaked. "That's what *you* think."

Chapter Eleven
Intergalactic

CHRIS WAS ABOUT to say, "What d'you mean?" when he noticed the old guy seemed to be crying. Adult tears always embarrassed him, so instead of asking that question he sighed, turned to Andy and asked another. "How come nobody's getting off?"

"How the heck should *I* know?" The kitten was becoming restless, trying to wriggle out of the top of Andy's jacket. Andy kept having to let go of the rail to block its escape, and every time he did so he nearly toppled over. "Ask 'em, if you want to know."

Oh yeah. Just like that, thought Chris. Excuse me, but isn't it about time some of you selfish prannocks got off and let me and my buddy sit down? Make me dead popular, that would. *I* could get off. Town can't be far now, and I'm fed up of this lot. Maybe the rain'll have stopped.

Chris tapped his companion on the shoulder. "Think I'll get off and walk from here. Coming?"

Andy shook his head. "No way. It must

be at least two miles and it's chucking it down."

"We've been going ages – it can't be anything like two miles. And the rain might have stopped."

"It hasn't. And if we were coming into Cranley there'd be lights. Street lights, house lights. I tell you we're miles out."

"I don't see how we *can* be," argued Chris. "It took us twenty-five minutes to get to Barmston, so it should be twenty-five minutes back. We got on at ten to six, so . . ." He looked at his watch. Ten to six. He shook his wrist. "Damn thing's stopped. What time is it by yours?"

"If I try to look I'll fall over. *You* look."

Chris craned his neck to see his companion's watch. Ten to six.

"Yours has stopped too," he told Andy.

"*Can't* have. It's a genuine fake Rolex. What time does it say?"

"Ten to six, same as mine."

"Then it *is* ten to six, dummy."

"No it's not. It was ten to six when we got on. I *looked*."

"It was dark. Rain in your eyes. You made a mistake."

"I did *not* make a mistake, Andy. We got on this bus at ten to six and both our watches stopped immediately. Something's wrong."

"Oh, sure." Andy smirked. "We've been kidnapped by aliens, Chris. This may *look* like a bus but it's really an intergalactic cruiser, and the reason we don't see lights out there is because we're in deep space."

"Don't!" Chris shivered. "This isn't a joke, Andy. Something *is* wrong."

"Cool it, kiddo," laughed Andy. "You'll have *me* freaking out next. Look. Our watches got wet, right? They stopped. We got a different bus, goes round another way, takes a bit longer. That's all." He gazed at the other boy. "That's *all*, Chris. OK?"

But it didn't *feel* OK.

Chapter Twelve
No Can Do

THE BUS RUMBLED on. They were still going downhill. Chris stared past the woman with the bag and the man next to her, who seemed to have nodded off. Mostly, the window was a black mirror reflecting the crowded saloon, but now and then he caught a glimpse of the outside – enough to see that they were in a narrow valley. The ground rose steeply on either side. There seemed to be no houses on the slopes because there were no lights. The rain-sodden sky was so dark that you couldn't see where the slopes ended and the sky began – there was no horizon.

Chris was seriously worried now. In fact he was scared. They certainly hadn't travelled up this valley on the outward trip. Of course Andy could be right. The bus might be taking a different route, but in that case why were there no houses? No stops? Why wasn't anybody getting off?

And what about the driver and the guy with the badge? Stuff they said. The driver: *This'll take you where you're bound, lad.* Not, *Yes, we're off to Cranley.* And then he says: *Plenty of time to smoke when you get off*, and that sets the giggler off laughing. Why? What's funny about that? And then the old nutcase: *Ask the driver for another chance.* Another chance of *what*, for pete's sake? Chris wondered. And why did the giggler kill himself laughing when I asked if he'd moved somewhere a bit warmer?

Somewhere a bit warmer? Chris was thinking about that when something caught his eye. Something bright, sliding slowly across the window from right to left. A light, out there on the hillside. Well, no, not a light exactly. A *source* of light, but flickering. A fire, then. A small fire, in somebody's garden perhaps. In *this* rain?

Chris jogged Andy's elbow, pointing. Andy looked and nodded.

"There was another. Couple of minutes back. Bonfires."

Chris looked at him. "Bonfires *where*, Andy? *Whose* bonfires? There are no houses."

"Oh, for goodness' sake!" Andy rolled his eyes upward. "OK, Chris, they're not bonfires. They're . . . let's see . . . yeah, that's it — they're *comets*, right? We're six thousand million miles from Earth, surrounded by comets. Does that make you *feel* better, kiddo?"

Chris shook his head. "No it doesn't, Andy. It doesn't make me feel better at all. We may not be in space, but this bus isn't going to Cranley. We'd have been there ages ago. I'm getting off."

Andy shrugged, one hand clamped over the lump in his jacket. "Suit yourself. I'll see you Monday in school."

Chris turned and shuffled forward. The driver was staring straight ahead, his hands clamped on the wheel. Chris looked at him. "Excuse me?"

"Can't," grunted the man, without turning his head.

"Wh – what d'you mean, *can't*? I want to get off."

"Can't excuse you. Not my job. I just drive this thing."

"Well I *know* that. I want the next stop, please."

"Terminus, next stop."

"Cranley, you mean?"

"Cranley? Didn't say nothing about Cranley."

"Yes you did — when we got on. My friend asked and you said —"

"What?" The driver still didn't turn his head. Through the windshield, Chris watched light from their headlamps race along a fissured rockface. The valley had narrowed, its sides soaring so steeply it was like driving in a tunnel. Here and there on the precipitous slopes, fires flickered. The driver blinked. "*What* did I say?"

"You said, *This'll take you where you're bound.*"

The man nodded. "No mention of Cranley."

"No, but . . . ?"

"What?"

"Well — that's where we're bound. Cranley."

The driver shook his head. "Not your friend. He's bound for a different place altogether."

"But . . . he lives in Cranley, same as me. We're at school together."

"I know that."

"Well then, let us off if you're not going to Cranley."

The man shook his head. "Sorry, kiddo. No can do."

Chapter Thirteen
Another Comedian

"Andy?"

"What now?"

"We're not off home. The driver's just told me."

"So – why're you still here? You said you were getting off."

"He won't *let* me. Terminus next stop, he says."

"And where's that?"

"I didn't ask."

"Dork." Andy shoved the kitten's head down. "Well, wherever it is, we'll catch a bus to Cranley from there. Remember:

> Got my ticket
> Paid my fare
> Where it takes me
> I don't care."

"But *I* do," gulped Chris. "I'm *scared*, Andy. I don't recognise any of the places we're passing, and I've been everywhere with Mum and Dad. This terminus – it must be miles away. What if there *are* no buses back? I want you to talk to the driver. Get him to stop."

Andy gazed at him. "Then what? Suppose he *does* stop, and we get off here in the middle of nowhere. What do we do – hitch it back to Barmston?"

"*Yes.* That'd do for me, Andy. Anything, just so we get off this rotten bus."

Andy sighed. "OK. I'll have a word if you'll hold this for me." He unzipped his jacket and pulled out the kitten. Chris held it against his chest with his free hand. It clung on, shivering. He could feel the prick of its tiny claws through his shirt. Andy zipped up and squeezed past.

He was back in a minute, looking peeved. "What a plonker," he snarled. "What a miserable old wassock." He shook his head. "He won't stop, won't say where we're going, won't tell me how far it is. All he'd say was, there are no buses back."

"I *knew* it," cried Chris. "I *knew* we were gonna get stuck somewhere we didn't want to be." Tears started down his cheeks and he hadn't a hand to wipe them with.

The giggler whooped again. "Somewhere we didn't want . . . ooooh, ha ha ha . . ."

Outside, the valley was growing narrower, the soaring hillsides more precipitous. There were so many fires now that a single window would frame three or four simultaneously, and in their ruddy glow Chris thought he glimpsed figures dancing. As the bus descended the temperature climbed. There was a sulphurous smell, like matches.

"Andy." Chris plucked at his companion's sleeve. "I . . . I think I know where the bus is going." He was crying, not bothering to conceal it.

Andy shrugged, forced a grin. "Yeah, I reckon I do too. Bummer, eh?"

"Is that all you can *say*?" It came out as a scream.

Andy pulled a face. "What d'you *want* me to say . . . that I didn't know you could go that far on a Day Rover?"

"You could . . . you . . . I don't know. You don't seem to *care*. I wish . . . I wish I'd gone to the garden centre with Mum and Dad. I wish . . ."

"You wish," sneered Andy. "You make me puke with your wishes, kiddo. If wishes were horses, beggars would ride, as my old granny never used to say."

"Ask," rattled a voice behind him. "You know – what I said before." Chris turned. The old man's watery eyes seemed to implore.

"Go *on*, lad – your mate deserves to be on this ride and so do I, but you don't, so *ask*."

"Yes," Chris nodded. "Yes, I will. Thanks."

Behind him Andy laughed, a mirthless bark. "Save your breath to cool your . . ."

The giggler's whoop drowned out the rest. "Save your breath to cool . . . to cool . . . ooooh. I don't *believe* it – *another* comedian." Overwhelmed, the escort lost his hold on the rail and fell to the floor where he lay like a comma among the legs, seismic with laughter.

Chris turned and staggered to the

platform. The driver was a blur beyond his tears. "Please," he choked, "another chance. One more. I swear . . ."

Chapter Fourteen
Someone Else's Dream

"BAD COMPANY," GRUNTED the driver, keeping his eyes on the road. Chris knuckled his eyes with one hand, clutched the kitten with the other. "M—me?"

"Naw!" The man shook his head.

"T'other un." He sighed. "We're stuck with our families but we can choose our friends. You made a poor choice, lad."

"And you think I deserve to go to . . . to . . . just for *that*?"

The driver shot him a glance. "Not really. You needed the frightener, that's all."

"Frightener?" Hope flickered.

"Yep." The man shifted slightly in his seat. Brakes squealed. The bus slowed. Chris stared. "You mean – you're letting me *off*?"

The driver nodded. "This time. But if you ever catch my bus again it's a one-way ticket to the terminus."

Chris shook his head, giddy with relief. "I won't catch it again, mister. I *mean* it."

"I know you do." The vehicle squeaked to a halt and stood juddering. The door hissed open, admitting a blast of air so hot it stung. The acrid stench of sulphur made him gag. The driver regarded him levelly. "Not very nice, is it, Christopher?"

"N – no."

"Well, let me tell you, this is nothing, lad – *nothing*, compared to what it's like at the terminus." He nodded towards the kitten. "What about that?"

"I'll take it back to the shop."

"Good." The engine revved. "Off you go, then."

Chris glanced towards Andy, who was watching him through sad eyes, then at the driver. "Any chance of . . . ?"

"None at all. I'd go if I were you,

unless you've changed your mind."

Chris stood on the sticky tarmac, gazing after the bus. Heat warped the vehicle out of shape, like looking at it underwater. He could see where the overarching crags finally met to form a tunnel and as he watched, the tunnel swallowed the bus. He sighed and turned, holding the kitten to his heart. As he set off uphill he was assailed by a feeling of unreality, like a figure in the landscape of someone else's dream.

DISCOVER . . .

SURFERS

. . . FAST PACY READS

The following SURFERS *titles are available:*

DEEP WATER by Ann Turnbull

THE JOKE SHOP by Ian Strachan

MAD MYTHS: STONE ME!

by Steve Barlow & Steve Skidmore

MOVE OVER, EINSTEIN! by Margaret Springer

MUTINY IN SPACE by Cherith Baldry